THE
AFGHANISTAN WAR

BY MAX WINTER

Published by The Child's World®
1980 Lookout Drive • Mankato, MN 56003-1705
800-599-READ • www.childsworld.com

ACKNOWLEDGMENTS
The Child's World®: Mary Berendes, Publishing Director
Red Line Editorial: Editorial direction
The Design Lab: Design
Amnet: Production
Content Consultant: Thomas E. Gouttierre, Director, Center for
Afghanistan Studies, University of Nebraska Omaha

Photographs ©: U.S. Army, cover; Glenn Fawcett, 4;
The Design Lab, 5; Amber Robinson/U.S. Army, 7;
Department of Defense, 8, 12, 21; Dan Howell/Shutterstock
Images, 9; Brennan Linsley/AP Images, 10; Richard Drew/AP
Images, 13; Al Jazeera/AP Images, 14; Thinkstock, 15; Spc.
David Marck Jr./U.S. Army, 16; J. Scott Applewhite/AP
Images, 19; Aqeel Ahmed/AP Images, 22; Staff Sgt. Teddy Wade,
25; Spc. Gregory Argentieri, 27; Susan Walsh/AP Images, 28

Design Element: Shutterstock Images

ISBN 9781631437120
LCCN 2014945405

Printed in the United States of America
Mankato, MN
November, 2014
PA02243

ABOUT THE AUTHOR

Max Winter has written several books on nonfiction subjects. He was living in New York City on September 11, 2001.

TABLE OF CONTENTS

★ ★ ★

CHAPTER ONE

A MORNING BATTLE

★ ★ ★

Clinton Romesha was a staff sergeant in the U.S. Army. He was stationed at Combat Outpost Keating in Afghanistan in October 2009. It was years since the Afghanistan War began. On the morning of October 3, Romesha and his fellow soldiers awoke to an attack. Enemy soldiers surrounded their camp. The attacking soldiers fired their weapons. Romesha helped lead the U.S. troops to safety so they would survive.

Clinton Romesha

The Afghanistan War started in 2001. A group called al-Qaeda attacked the United States. They crashed four planes on U.S. soil.

UNITED STATES

AFGHANISTAN

N
NW   NE
W   E
SW   SE
S

The United States sent troops to Afghanistan in search of the **terrorists**. They were hiding in Afghanistan. Fast forward eight years, and the biggest battles of the war had stopped. But small fights started all the time. U.S. troops were needed to help keep the peace.

Romesha called for backup. While he waited for help, he walked into enemy fire. He wanted to find out where the enemy was hiding. The U.S. soldiers needed to be in a safer position. Many were injured and some soldiers had been killed.

COMBAT OUTPOST KEATING

Combat Outpost Keating was a small U.S. military station. It was built in a remote location in Afghanistan. Because it lay in a mountain valley, it was difficult to defend. Approximately 60 troops were stationed here. The battle that took place at the outpost is considered by many historians to be a symbol. It represents the great difficulty of the Afghanistan War.

Romesha and other soldiers prevented the **Taliban**, the group that was trying to occupy Afghanistan, from taking the soldiers' bodies. Romesha's courage made it possible for the United States to claim and secure Combat Outpost Keating. This battle was over. But the bigger fight was not. Romesha and thousands of other U.S. troops would stay in Afghanistan for a few more years, fighting the Taliban.

A helicopter lands at Combat Outpost Keating in Afghanistan after the battle in 2009.

ANOTHER **V**IEW

What if you were one of the troops under Romesha's command? How would you feel about his actions that day? How would you feel about being in combat?

CHAPTER TWO

HOW THE WAR BEGAN

★ ★ ★

O n September 11, 2001, four passenger airplanes crashed in the United States. Terrorists had **hijacked** the airplanes. Two of the planes crashed into the World Trade Center buildings in New York City. A third plane crashed into the Pentagon in Washington, DC. The fourth plane crashed in a field in Pennsylvania. Nearly 3,000 people died. Many consider this the worst attack on U.S. soil since the bombing of Pearl Harbor by the Japanese in 1941. That event caused the United States to enter World War II (1939–1945).

George W. Bush

Smoke pours from the World Trade Center buildings after hijacked planes crashed into them. ▶

President George W. Bush and other U.S. leaders wanted to respond. But they needed to confirm who was responsible for the airplane hijackings. The U.S. government found out the group was called al-Qaeda. Members of the group hid in Afghanistan, a country in the Middle East. But Taliban leaders would not reveal the group's location. The Taliban ruled Afghanistan from 1996 to 2001. With no answers from Afghan leaders, the United States began secret missions to Afghanistan in late September 2001.

U.S. soldiers had to take control of Afghanistan away from the Taliban.

The purpose of the missions was to capture al-Qaeda members. U.S. soldiers wanted to prevent further violence. After beginning a bombing campaign on October 7, 2001,

U.S. soldiers took control of Afghanistan's capital, Kabul.

On November 13, the Taliban retreated without military response. But this was only the beginning of a very long war.

THE TALIBAN

The Taliban is a religious group. Its members follow **Islam**. The group has strict rules. Men are required to wear beards. Girls older than ten are not allowed to go to school. When women leave their homes, they must wear dark robes. The robes cover their whole bodies. They even cover their faces. The Taliban does not allow music, movies, or television. But not everyone in Afghanistan liked the strict rules of the Taliban.

ANOTHER VIEW

Firefighters helped pull Americans from the rubble of the destroyed buildings on September 11, 2001. They had to be careful because the rubble was unstable. The air at the site was also believed to be unsafe to breathe. But the firefighters went anyway. They wanted to save lives. Imagine you were a rescue worker that day. How would you feel?

CHAPTER THREE

THE LONG STRUGGLE

★ ★ ★

Hamid Karzai

After U.S. troops forced the Taliban out of Kabul, Afghanistan had no leaders. The United Nations (UN) held a conference. The UN is an organization of countries from around the world. This group works to make global decisions. At the conference in 2001, the UN decided that a local leader of tribes, Hamid Karzai, would be the country's temporary leader.

In early 2002, the United States began searching for al-Qaeda's leaders. They wanted to find three central figures. These included Osama bin Laden, Ayman al-Zawahiri,

World leaders met at the 2001 UN conference to decide who would rule Afghanistan. ▶

Osama bin Laden made video announcements from an unknown hiding place.

and Mohammed Omar. Without much help, it was difficult to find where they were hiding.

Afghanistan is a rocky, mountainous country that is full of caves. Bin Laden was the primary target. Experts thought he could be hiding in the caves of Tora Bora. These caves were in Afghanistan, near the border with Pakistan.

Omar and al-Zawahiri had settled there, along with other al-Qaeda officials. But the United States did not have enough information stating Bin Laden was there, too.

Before the Afghanistan War, women held a very low social position in Afghanistan. Under Taliban rule, women had very few freedoms. They also had little say in their country's political developments. After the war began, things changed. Some women served in the Afghanistan military force. They helped push back Taliban forces. And later, after the Taliban had been overthrown, women held public office. While men and women were still not entirely equal under new rule, important changes were taking place. Imagine you were a woman in Afghanistan, gaining new rights and freedoms. What would you have to say about these changes?

The U.S. military fought on the ground and by air in Operation Anaconda.

Although U.S. troops searched for the leaders, they still could not find them. In March 2002, approximately 800 al-Qaeda soldiers fought U.S. troops in a battle called Operation Anaconda. Three U.S. **battalions**, along with 300 Afghan soldiers, attacked al-Qaeda forces. The United States thought this battle would be a brief. U.S. troops believed they were better prepared than the enemy. However, the battle lasted two weeks. It is generally not considered a U.S. victory because of the high number of casualties. As the United States began to realize the mission would be a challenge, other countries were brought into the conflict. These countries offered additional troops and equipment. Among the countries were the United Kingdom, Canada, and Australia. These countries were members of a peacemaking group of nations called the North Atlantic Treaty Organization (NATO).

NATO

NATO is a group of 28 countries. They join together to support and defend each other in times of military conflict. NATO was formed in 1949. The goal of the organization is to ensure that peace is maintained throughout the world. When conflicts begin, the members have clear and reasonable discussions about military actions to take. Throughout its history, NATO has helped keep the world safe in wartime.

CHAPTER FOUR

THE ONGOING WAR

★ ★ ★

The war continued, slowly but violently, throughout 2002. The United States gave money to Afghanistan to rebuild. But it wasn't always enough. From 2003 forward, the war progressed unevenly. At some points the war seemed to be over. Then another battle would occur. On May 1, 2003, President George W. Bush announced the Afghanistan War was over. The United States began to pull troops out of Afghanistan. The number of U.S. troops left was 9,000. This was a small amount from the start of the war.

In 2004, Afghanistan held its first **democratic** election. The country also elected its first **parliament**. Although the country had become more stable, the war was far from over.

President George W. Bush pulled troops out of Afghanistan and moved them to Iraq to fight a new conflict. ▶

The Taliban began to gain strength again in Afghanistan in 2005. It had new fighting methods. The worst of these methods was suicide bombing. Suicide bombers went to crowded places and blew themselves up with explosives. These attacks could be extremely destructive.

HAMID KARZAI

Hamid Karzai was Afghanistan's leader from 2004 to 2014. He had been active in his country's politics since he was a young man. When the Taliban first arrived in Afghanistan, Karzai supported them. Gradually he became less supportive. He didn't like their strict policies. During his presidency, Karzai faced resistance from two directions. Fighting against the Taliban strained his ability to lead. And Afghan people saw him as weak. Ashraf Ghani was sworn in as the new president of Afghanistan in September 2014.

A vehicle explosion took place in 2006. Several military personnel were killed. NATO then took over the conflict. Countries other than the United States now fought the war in Afghanistan. But U.S. troops continued looking for Osama bin Laden and other al-Qaeda members.

Osama bin Laden had been a major target of the United States since 2001. The United States hunted for him from Afghanistan to Pakistan with no luck. In the years following the initial search for bin Laden, the United States killed many al-Qaeda officials.

Hamid Karzai was elected Afghanistan's first president.

After many years of hunting, U.S. troops found Osama bin Laden hiding in this compound in Pakistan.

But U.S. troops had not found bin Laden himself. Finally on May 1, 2011, a U.S. Special Forces team was sent to Abbottabad, Pakistan. Intelligence sources were fairly certain bin Laden was hiding in a **compound** there. This new information came from an **informant**. U.S. forces raided the compound at night. In a brief but intense gun battle, U.S. troops killed bin Laden.

Many consider bin Laden's death the end of the war in Afghanistan. In the years following bin Laden's death, Afghanistan has endured much hardship. It has also worked to rebuild itself.

ANOTHER VIEW

Wars have taken place for centuries in Pakistan, Iraq, and Afghanistan. The United States has not experienced continuous warfare like that. Try to think what life would be like in one of these countries during the war. How would daily activities take place there? What would the difficulties be?

CHAPTER FIVE

REBUILDING AFGHANISTAN

★ ★ ★

Although Afghanistan was greatly damaged by the war, the conflict helped begin the process of rebuilding the country. Some of these developments improved the quality of life for Afghan citizens. Others did not. While there are still foreign troops stationed in Afghanistan, the full battle has ended.

As the war drew to a close, Afghanistan's government needed a lot of work. The change to a democratic government gave citizens a voice. But the Taliban challenged the system regularly. The Taliban have continued to gain strength in Afghanistan. Ongoing

A U.S. soldier stops during his patrol to talk with an Afghan construction worker. ▶

combat between the Taliban and the government has taken many lives. More than 60,000 Afghan people have died as a result of the war. The citizens of Afghanistan continue to disagree about how the country should be led.

The economy is very unstable. Many of the country's people live in poverty. The average yearly income of an Afghan citizen is very low by modern standards. Much of the economy of the country depends on illegal activities, such as drug sales. Many people work in agriculture. But more than a third of the country's population is unemployed.

Education has improved in the country as a result of the changes in government. Education has become far more important in Afghanistan than it was before the war. The government has built 4,000 schools since 2002.

POWER IN AFGHANISTAN

One result of the Afghanistan War is that much of the country was left without electrical power for long stretches of time. Those who had electricity only had it in short bursts. Over the years, plans have been made to change that. The United States Agency for International Development (USAID) has begun one program. The goal of the program is to combine all of the power grids in Afghanistan into one grid. This will help provide steady power for everyone in the country.

More than 50 percent of school-age children are now enrolled in Afghan schools. These students received new book bags and school supplies as part of school partnership program.

President Barack Obama spoke in 2014 about withdrawing most U.S. troops from Afghanistan by the end of 2016.

More than 175,000 teachers have received training. This is a huge leap from before the war.

Wars have occurred throughout history. They will continue to occur all over the world. The Afghanistan War was long and complicated. It resulted in many casualties. However, it caused important changes in Afghanistan. History will tell what the results of those changes will be.

Daily life for Afghan people has been difficult. There has been very little electricity or running water in major cities and towns in the country. Pretend you are living in Afghanistan. Can you imagine living in a small country that has been at war for more than ten years? How would you handle having limited food supplies?

TIMELINE

September 11, 2001 | Al-Qaeda terrorists crash four U.S. passenger airplanes in the United States, killing thousands of Americans.

November 2001 | The Taliban is forced to leave Kabul when U.S. forces take control of the city.

March 2002 | Operation Anaconda, one of the war's bloodiest battles, takes place in Afghanistan.

May 1, 2003 | The United States declares the Afghanistan War over.

December 7, 2004 | Hamid Karzai becomes the first president of Afghanistan.

September 8, 2006 | Several Pakistani and U.S. soldiers are killed in the suicide bombing of a military vehicle, causing NATO to take over the situation.

May 1, 2011 | Osama bin Laden is killed in a compound in Pakistan.

May 27, 2014 | President Barack Obama announces plans to withdraw most U.S. troops by 2016.

GLOSSARY

battalions (buh-AL-yuns) Battalions are large organized groups of soldiers. U.S. battalions moved into Afghanistan during the war.

compound (KOM-pound) A compound is a fenced in area containing a group of buildings. Osama bin Laden was found hiding in a compound.

democratic (dem-uh-KRAT-ik) A democratic government is when people choose leaders by voting. Afghanistan had its first democratic election in 2004.

hijacked (HYE-jakd) An aircraft that has been hijacked has been taken by force. Terrorists hijacked four U.S. passenger planes in 2001.

informant (in-FOR-ment) An informant is a person who gives information. An informant let the United States known where bin Laden was hiding.

Islam (ISS-lahm) Islam is a religion that teaches there is only one God and that Muhammad is God's prophet. Muslims practice Islam.

parliament (PAR-luh-munt) A parliament is the group of people responsible for making laws in some governments. Afghanistan elected its first parliament in 2004.

Taliban (TAL-i-ban) The Taliban is an Islamic militia in Afghanistan. The Taliban tried to occupy Afghanistan.

terrorists (TER-ur-ists) Terrorists are people belonging to a group that uses violent acts to frighten people as a way to achieve a political goal. The United States went to Afghanistan in search of the terrorists responsible for September 11.

TO LEARN MORE

BOOKS

Fiscus, James W. *America's War in Afghanistan*. New York: Rosen Publishing, 2004.

Fradin, Dennis Brindell. *September 11, 2001*. Tarrytown, NY: Marshall Cavendish, 2010.

Owings, Lisa. *Afghanistan*. Minneapolis: Bellwether Media, 2011.

WEB SITES

Visit our Web site for links about the Afghanistan War: **childsworld.com/links**

Note to Parents, Teachers, and Librarians: We routinely verify our Web links to make sure
they are safe and active sites. So encourage your readers to check them out!

INDEX